This book is dedicated to Ivy Halting who is really nice and is going bowling on Saturday and can take a friend hint hint.

x X x

EGMONT

First published in paperback in Great Britain 2011
by Egmont UK Limited
The Yellow Building, 1 Nicholas Road
London, W11 4AN

Text copyright © 2011 Kjartan Poskitt
Illustrations copyright © 2011 David Tazzyman

The moral rights of the author and illustrator have been asserted

ISBN 978 1 4052 5596 7

1 3 5 7 9 10 8 6 4 2

www.egmont.co.uk

A CIP catalogue record for this title is available from the British Library

Printed and bound in Great Britain by the CPI Group (UK) Ltd, Croydon, CR0 4YY

47905/3

MIX
Paper
FSC FSC® C018306

EGMONT LUCKY COIN

Our story began over a century ago, when seventeen-year-old
Egmont Harald Petersen found a coin in the street.

He was on his way to buy a flyswatter, a small hand-operated
printing machine that he then set up in his tiny apartment.

The coin brought him such good luck that today Egmont has
offices in over 30 countries around the world. And that lucky
coin is still kept at the company's head offices in Denmark.

Agatha Parrot
and the FLOATING Head

Typed out neatly by
Kjartan Poskitt

Illustrated by David Tazzyman

EGMONT

The gang!

Arty **Bianca** likes painting wild animals and plays her trombone loud on Sunday mornings.

Big jolly **Martha** likes chips and football and can sort out boys anytime.

Agatha (that's me) is going to be a famous celebrity actress. And that's true.

Mad Ivy once did 103 hops on the same leg without stopping. Nobody knows why, not even her.

Ellie is scared of being in this book because she had a dream that the pages were squashing her.

Odd Street
Primary
School

ODD STREET

No 1	No 3	No 5	No 7	No 9
Bianca	Martha	Agatha	Ivy	Ellie

CONTENTS

The Usual Boring Old Warning

Hiya and THANKS for trying out this book! But before we get on to the story I've got to warn you about something.

1

It starts all nice and normal like this . . .

Last Tuesday me and Ivy went for tea at Martha's house.

. . . **BUT** there's a bit later on where Martha's head explodes. Don't worry because she's all right, even if one of the teachers was trying to chop her head off with an axe. It all ends up happily ever after with everybody having ice creams so is

2

that OK with you? Good.

Sorry about that, but the old man who is typing this book out for me says that you have to have SAFETY WARNINGS. To be honest I couldn't care if this book freaks you out so much that you have a nosebleed, in fact I think that'd be pretty cool (ha ha!) but he says I have to warn you about the Martha's head bit because if I didn't then you might ask me for £1000000000 of compensation but you'd be lucky because I've only got 73p so there. You have been warned.

There's still a couple of pages left before the story starts so I'll introduce myself because that's good manners.

I'm Agatha Jane Parrot and I'm a supermodel celebrity actress who just happens to be killing a bit of time at school before I get famous. Soon I'll be in films and having my picture in the papers and going to posh parties, but first I've got to learn all that stuff like the water cycle and the eight times table.

Yesterday we did the Romans invading Britain but I don't know why the Romans bothered. It was cold and wet and we hadn't even got any telly to watch in those days so

5

they might just as well have stayed in sunny Italy eating pizzas. Sounds good to me.

Me and Ivy and Martha all go to Odd Street School which is at the end of our street where we live which is called Odd Street because the houses just have odd numbers like 1, 3, 5, 7, 9, 11, 13, 15 . . . and all that lot.

If there were any houses on the other side of the street then they would be the even numbers, but there aren't.

Ivy says it's because somebody folded the plans in half and the builders didn't realise so they missed half the street off and I believe her ha ha! It's probably not the truth, but who cares so long as it's funny? My granny believes there's little sooty fairies living up her chimney and she's well cool so there.

I live at number 5 with big brother James (a bit older and a lot smellier), little sister Tilly (with a pink sparkly ballet dress, need I say more?) and two old slaves to obey all my orders (i.e. Mum and Dad) but none of them come into this story so don't bother remembering all that.

Next door at number 3 is Martha who is the big smiley one who can fight boys,

8

then on the other
side at number 7
is Ivy the hyper-
nutcase who always
jumps over her gate and swings off
the washing line. Yahoo GO IVY!

There's lots of other people
and stuff to know but you'll pick it
all up as the story goes along. As
well as Martha's head exploding
there's a balloon that gets top marks
in spelling and a mad teacher who

saves the world from a bit of wet carpet but first of all there's a really disgusting pizza. How disgusting? I'll give you a clue:

What would you get if you drove a steam roller along the bottom of the ocean?

Give in? Never mind, the answer's coming soon. Off we go then . . .

The Start

. . . .

Last Tuesday me and Ivy went to tea at Martha's house. Martha's mum works at the Spendless food shop and they have a slogan 'You'll spend less at Spendless' which is true. Most people go in, take one look round and then come

11

out without spending anything at all. That's because Spendless never sells anything you might have heard of, but the good bit is that Martha's mum gets lots of random things to bring home and try out.

That night Martha's mum put three uncooked cheese and tomato pizzas on the table then she opened up all her cupboards and

12

got out all the half-eaten pots and packets she could find. 'Choose your own toppings,' she said. 'Put on whatever you like!' Martha's mum is big and jolly just like Martha.

Most of the pots had labels with funny writing on them, so the only way to tell what was inside was by opening them up and having a look. The first one I tried turned out to be marmalade which isn't too bad on a pizza actually. I'd give it 6/10. Ivy found ham with red pepper bits (8/10), pineapple (10/10) and black cherries in syrup (2/10 but Ivy LOVES them because she's nuts).

We put loads of stuff on the pizzas. I made a spider pattern, Martha did a rainbow and Ivy did a face with lots of mad hair made from spaggetty. (Or is it spaggeti? Spaghety? Spahgetti . . . oh you know what I mean, it's that long stringy stuff you can eat with bollonays sauce. Bolonaiz. Bollonnaze . . . OH FORGET IT.) She said it was supposed to be me because my hair is a bit impossible like my mum's is.

At least it's better than having hair like my dad because he's as bald as a light bulb ha ha!

We'd just about finished loading up the pizzas when Martha opened a jar of yellowy-pink stuff which smelt like James's football socks (0/10).

'No way am I having THAT!' said Ivy.

'Coward,' said Martha.

'Then I dare you to put it on YOUR pizza,' said Ivy.

That got Martha thinking. 'I've already got pineapple, beetroot, garlic sausage, dried banana, olives and raspberry jam. Anything else might ruin the taste.'

I had a look at the label on the jar.

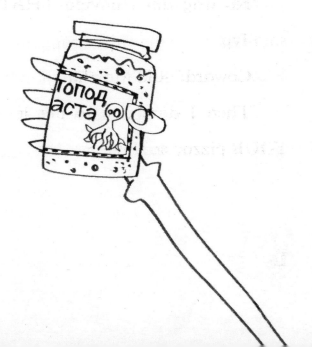

The only bit I could understand was the 'best before' date and it was ages away, so whatever it was should have been safe enough.

Ivy gave Martha a poke in the ribs. 'Go on Martha, I dare you to eat all that for a million billion pounds.'

Ha! Martha would eat her own head for 20p. So for a million billion pounds she slopped the whole jar of yellowy-pink stuff all over her pizza (oh boy did it STINK or what?), and then her mum came in and shoved all the pizzas in the oven.

We had ten minutes to wait, so we got talking about the class trip that was coming up. There were only three days left before half-term and so far not one person in our class had had a single day off sick. As a special reward Miss Pingle had said that if we all made it to the last day, the whole class would go to see the Egyptian mummy exhibition! Mummies are well cool because out of zombies, vampires and mummies, they are the only ones that are real. At least I think so. Gosh I hope so. **Eeky freak – scary!**

'I bet one of the boys goes off sick and ruins it,' said Martha crossly. 'Remember the end of last term when Matty knocked himself out playing football?'

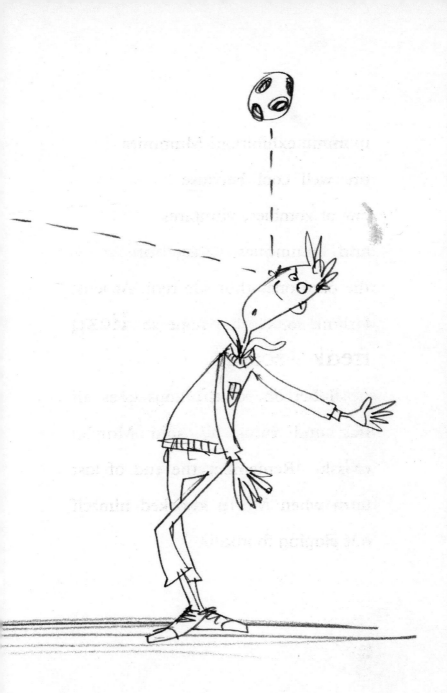

Hmmm . . . that wasn't how Ivy and I remembered it! Actually it was Martha who knocked Matty out. He'd kicked the football across the playground and hit Martha on the leg and messed her trousers up. All the boys had laughed so she kicked it back HARD and the next thing Matty knew he was sitting in reception with a bandage round his head. Ha ha wicked!

'It was still his fault,' said Martha. 'So if he does it again I'll kill him. Well, not kill him, but you know what I mean.'

Soon the pizzas were out of the oven and being chopped up and then Ivy was owing Martha a million billion pounds because Martha had eaten the lot. Then Martha's mum came in and saw the strange jar was empty.

'Aha!' she said, sounding a bit

surprised. 'I see you've finished off that octopus paste.'

'*Octopus paste*?' gasped Martha.

Ivy started giggling and doing a strange underwater dance round the kitchen. 'Whoa! Does that mean Martha might grow eight arms?'

Gosh, what a thought. Argh! Mind you, if Martha really did get eight arms, she'd be scarier than mummies, vampires and zombies all put together! Awesome.

Looking Down Plugholes

Next day and it's lunchtime, and we're all sitting round in the school hall. Our hall gets used for everything like concerts and football practice and assemblies, so there's tons of stuff round the sides like ropes for climbing up and folded tables and a plinky plonky piano and a projector thing that has a sign saying **CHILDREN MUST NOT TOUCH** but that's OK as it looks dead boring. It's not like it's a playstation or a chocolate bar machine or bubble blower is it?

There are also lots of piles of stacked up chairs. You're only meant to have five chairs stacked up at the most but Motley the caretaker likes to make things more exciting.

That morning he had made a giant wobbly pile of NINE chairs! I expect the world record for stacking chairs is something like twenty-two or maybe even twenty-three because if the pile got any higher then you'd need to have a hole in the ceiling. But nine is pretty good for Motley, it might even be his personal best so let's have a round of applause for Motley clap clap clap.

So anyway, me and Ivy were just quietly sandwiching away when **CRASH**. Rory Bloggs had been running and slipped on a biscuit wrapper and smashed his big head into Motley's nine stacking chairs which all fell on him ha ha. He was lying on the floor groaning and clutching his knee. Of course me and Ivy ignored him, but then something really bad happened. Miss Barking turned up.

Miss Barking has got short black hair and big glasses like telly screens and she always carries a thick folder full of boring leaflets and forms to fill in. We hardly ever see her in school because she's the deputy headteacher and she's always away learning about *issues*. Issues can be anything so long as it's boring and wastes time. Once she spent three days in a hotel learning about *nutritional issues*, then she came back to give us all a talk about not eating crisps for breakfast. Honestly, she shouldn't go giving us ideas. The very next morning Martha swapped her cornflakes for a monster packet of cheese and onion crisps and said it was great, although you have to eat them fast before the milk makes them go floppy.

Miss Barking stared at Rory then she stared at the biscuit wrapper, and then what does she do? Does she get the first aid kit?

No. Does she call the ambulance? No. Does she have him stretchered off into a waiting helicopter like they do in films? NO! She opens her folder and starts hunting for a special biscuit-wrapper-accident form.

'I *knew* this would happen one day,' she moaned at Rory, who was still on the floor making a big fuss. 'I told Mrs Twelvetrees that all biscuit wrappers should be removed by trained members of staff in a secure environment, but does she ever listen to me?'

That didn't get an answer. Partly because it was such a silly question but mainly because nobody was listening. She never learns.

Rory was just about to make an even bigger fuss but he was in our class, so Ivy and me realised we better do something. We pulled him up to his feet and held him by the arms.

'He's fine,' I said.

'But I must take him to the office to be checked,' said Miss Barking. 'He'll need an accident report, and then he'll have to go home.'

'No way,' said Ivy shaking her head. 'He just needs a quick run round the playground to loosen up, don't you Rory?'

Rory was shaking his head stupidly.

'Oh, so you *don't* need a run?' said Ivy. 'That's good, isn't it Miss Barking? He must be better already.'

Good one Ivy! The two of us dragged Rory away from Miss Barking. He was pretending to limp because he thought we'd feel sorry for him. He thought wrong.

'Walk properly,' hissed Ivy. 'She's watching, and if she sends you home, we won't get to see the mummies.'

'You're lucky Martha's not here,' I said. 'She'd have made you run round the playground.'

Rory shook us off him and stomped away. He was sulking so much he forgot to limp ha ha big loser!

But then we realised, where was Martha? She had never missed lunchtime before. We asked around and in the end it was Bianca Bayuss who told us with a very serious face:

'She was toiling to the runnets.'

We love Bianca. Don't always

understand her, but love her. Try
again Bianca . . .

'She was tunning to the roylets.'

Eh? Yikes! No wonder Bianca
was serious. She was trying to tell
us Martha was *running to the toilets.*
Ivy and me went to check and there
was Martha leaning her face over a
washbasin. She wasn't looking well,
so we were hoping that nobody else
had seen her, but we were too late.
There was somebody else already

in there. Gwendoline Tutt.

Gwendoline lives on Odd Street too, but she's in one of the big houses up at the far end. It should be number 59 but that's not posh enough for the Tutt family. They had to give their house a name instead. Are you ready for this? *Tomen Sbwriel*. Apparently her mum saw it on a sign in Wales and liked the sound of it which is a bit weird because the rest of us can't even say it.

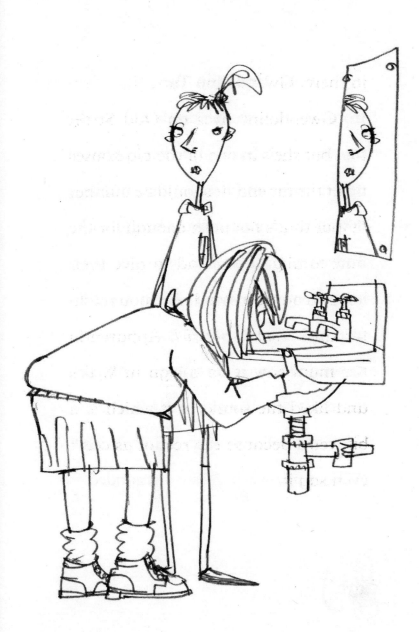

Gwendoline is in the other class from us so she wasn't getting to see the mummies and so she had been in a real mood all week. Typical Gwendoline, it was her fault anyway because she had been the one to miss a week off school when she went skiing while we were stuck in lessons. All the same, Gwendoline was the one who moaned the most because she was like that.

Gwendoline was staring at Martha. 'What's up with her?' she demanded.

'Nothing,' I said. I couldn't let Gwendoline know Martha was sick! I had to think of a good excuse. 'She just likes looking down plugholes, don't you Martha? In fact so do I.' I shoved my face in the next basin. 'Oooh, that's a nice one.'

Ivy stuck her head in a basin too. 'Mine's even better!' she said, but then being Ivy she had to go a bit mad. 'Oh wow that's soooo cool, love it love it love it.'

'You weirdos,' said Gwendoline but then she pulled a face and left thank goodness.

We got Martha standing up straight but her face was looking a bit green which wasn't good. If anyone found out she was ill then she'd be sent home and we'd miss our day out.

'I bet I know why you're woozy Martha,' said Ivy. 'It's that octopus paste isn't it? Go on, admit it. Octopus octopus octopus . . .'

44

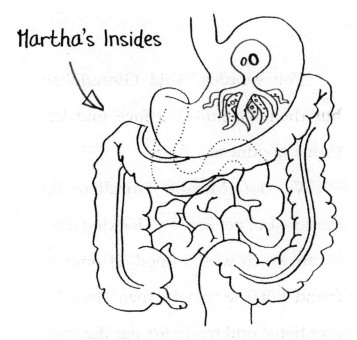

Martha's Insides

Martha was looking even greener but Ivy wouldn't shut up. 'Just imagine having a lot of chopped up octopus arms inside you!'

45

Martha's eyes were rolling and I was having to hold her up which was hard work because Martha's quite a healthy size if you know what I mean. 'Stop it Ivy!' I said, but she started waving her arms around excitedly.

'Hey, what if they all came alive at once? Blodge bubble blop blop blop . . .'

Whooops! Martha stuck her head straight back into the basin.

'Brilliant,' said Ivy. 'If she's sick

then I won't owe her a million billion pounds any more.'

'You big ninny,' I said. 'If a teacher sees her, they'll send her home. Quick, watch the door.'

Ivy whizzed off to keep a look-out while I splashed a bit of cold water in Martha's face. Eventually she straightened up again and took a few deep breaths.

'That was close!' she gasped. 'Sorry.'

'Don't worry about it,' I told her. 'We just need to get you through the afternoon. I've got an idea but we'll need help.'

The Cold
Heatwave

. . . .

By the time lessons had started, Ivy had got round all the other girls and told them what was going on and what they had to do. I helped Martha into class and sat her in Ellie Slippins's seat by the window but Miss Pingle didn't notice.

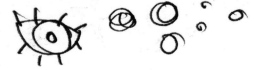

She's a new teacher and she's really good because her hair changes colour every week, and she can never work the computer. She was busy having a panic because the electronic white board was showing a poem about acorns when she needed to do times tables. She didn't notice that Martha was going green again.

'Please can we open the window?' I asked.

'What for?' she asked. (This week's

hair colour = deep orange by the way. Very nice too.)

'We're so hot,' I said.

'Hot? Really?' Miss P looked up and saw all the girls mopping their foreheads and gasping for air. Ivy was leaning right back in her chair fanning herself with her spelling book which was taking it a bit far, but that's Ivy for you. Anyway Miss P has only been out of college a year so she's still bright-eyed and

trusting bless her.

'All this hotness must be that global warming you were teaching us about,' I said. 'And you were absolutely right. You're such a good teacher.'

'Am I?' asked Miss Pingle looking very pleased.

'You must be, because we're boiling, aren't we?' said Ivy. All the girls nodded, but the boys just looked shocked.

'I'm cold,' said Matty.

'Me too,' said Liam and the other boys.

'Then you should cuddle up to keep warm,' said Ivy and the girls all laughed.

'URGHHHHH!' said all the boys. 'We're not that cold.'

'So can we have the window open a bit?' I asked.

'I suppose so,' said Miss Pingle and that's when she noticed Martha in Ellie's seat. 'Why have you two swapped?'

Ellie isn't very good at talking to teachers, so she just blushed. Ivy butted in and said, 'Ellie saw a massive SPIDER on the window sill and she didn't want to be wrapped up in a giant cobweb and EATEN ALIVE so she asked Martha to swap. Isn't that right Ellie?'

Ellie nodded and blushed even more.

'It must have been a *very* big spider,' muttered Miss Pingle.

Soon the window was open and Martha was sitting in a blast of cold fresh air and feeling a lot better.

Ivy leant over towards me and whispered, 'This global warming is freezing me to death! Let's hope Martha's back to normal tomorrow.'

But she wasn't.

Cornflakes and Eskimos

Next morning Ivy knocked on my door then we went to knock on number 3 to make sure Martha was up and ready for school.

'I'm sorry,' said Martha's mum, standing on the doorstep. 'But I really can't let her out. Could you take a note in for Miss Pingle?'

'Oh, she can't be that bad,' said Ivy.

'She didn't sleep at all last night,' said Martha's mum. 'She can't go to school. Come inside while I write the note.'

We went into the hall and waited while Martha's mum hurried off to the kitchen to find something to write on. Just then Martha came walking down the stairs in her pyjamas.

'Hi Martha!' I said. 'You look fine. Come on, get dressed, we'll wait for you.'

'Hi Dad,' said Martha, and she was looking at Ivy! 'Aren't cornflakes funny?'

'Eh?' said Ivy.

'Martha, it's us!' I said.

'I left my shoes on when I went swimming,' said Martha. 'Good job the octopus was asleep.'

'Octopus?' said Ivy sounding

worried. 'Is she growing

eight arms after all?'

'No!' I said. 'She's having

a joke and it's really funny. Hey

Martha, wait till the other kids

at school see your dizzy act,

they'll love it. So

come on, skirt, shirt,

shoes, school bag

and let's be

going . . .'

'But I have to count the oysters,' said Martha. 'Or they'll start to sing.'

Martha was starting to freak us a bit. I took hold of her hand and lifted it up but it was all floppy. When I let it go it just dropped back down again.

'Well, I better get ready for the eskimos,' said Martha and then she disappeared back upstairs again. Weird!

Then Martha's mum came back and said 'I'm sorry you can't see Martha. She's only just fallen asleep. In fact she was sleepwalking just before you called.'

Sleepwalking! That explained everything. Martha's mum held a note out for us to take, but that was no good! We HAD to get Martha into school someway, somehow . . .

I found myself pulling my hair which is what I do to wake my brain up. It works too! I'd just had an idea. It was a bit mad, but it had to be worth a try. 'Sorry,' I said to Martha's mum. 'I've just realised all my pockets are completely full, and so are yours Ivy. That's a pity, there's no room for the note, unless . . .'

'Unless what?' asked Martha's mum.

'Can I take Martha's coat?'

Martha's new coat was hanging up on the hall pegs. It was the most famous coat in the school because it was quite long and bright blue with yellow spots, and best of all it had a big hood. You'll see why that's important in a minute.

'I just need it for today. Then I can keep the note in the pocket, and what's more, if I'm carrying Martha's coat I'll remember to pass the note over. It's how my brain works, you see?'

Martha's mum looked surprised. 'Well, if you think it's necessary . . .'

'Absolutely vital,' I said and took the coat down off the hook. 'We'll see it comes back, promise!'

And then if you were watching us ten minutes later, you'd have seen me and Ivy walking into school, and in between us was Martha in her famous coat with her arms round our shoulders. At least, that's what it looked like. Ho ho, the mystery thickens. **Da-da-DAHHHH!**

Martha's Bummy is a Talloon

. . . .

Ivy was having a good old panic in the cloakroom. 'Oh no. Oh no. Oh no. Oh no. We'll never get away with this!' she kept saying. 'Oh no. Oh no . . .'

'Yes we will,' I told her. 'Won't we, Martha?'

The Martha in the blue and yellow coat didn't say anything. That's because her head was a balloon with a face on it, but with the hood pulled right over and a scarf round the neck, you could hardly see it! Awesome. I'd had to pinch the duvet off brother James's bed to fill the body out because as you know by now Martha is quite a healthy size (i.e. she's only about one pie off total fatness). We'd made the legs by stuffing my spare trousers with Dad's old newspapers. I checked that the gloves were still safely pinned on to the ends of the sleeves and Ivy made sure the shoes tied on to the legs weren't going to fall off. Bianca came in to hang her coat up. This was the first proper test!

'Hello Martha,' she said without looking round. 'Are you beeling fetter?'

I put my arm around Martha's shoulders like we were being mates.

70

'You mean feeling better?' I said.
'Yeah, Martha's fine, she's just lost
her voice, haven't you Martha?' I
stuck my ear in front of the balloon's
face and then nodded to pretend I
was listening. 'What's that? Oh yes
Martha, I'm sure they'll let you keep
your coat on. In fact it is a bit chilly,
so we'll all keep our coats on.'

Bianca looked amazed. 'I'm not
billy, I'm choiling!'

Of course she meant she was

71

boiling, but that was no good for our plan. 'Sorry Bianca. You can't be boiling today. Today you feel cold.'

'Cold?' asked Bianca. 'Why?'

Ivy gave me a prod in the ribs. It was the sort of prod which said 'we'll have to tell Bianca what we're doing.' I had to agree with the prod because Bianca sat next to Martha in class. Ivy went to keep guard by the door, then I unzipped the front of Martha's coat.

'Martha's bummy is a talloon?' gasped Bianca.

'Shhh!' I said. 'No, her head is a balloon, her tummy is a duvet. The real Martha's off sick, but we have to make the teachers think she's at school or we'll miss the trip. This is the Other Martha who's going to take her place today. Obviously she needs to keep her coat on and her hood up, so that's why we all need to pretend it's cold.'

Good old Bianca, she immediately put her coat back on, then Ellie Slippins came in and when we told her the plan, she kept her coat on too. Poor Ellie. She's always nervous at the best of times, so anything like this really freaks her out.

'Everything will be fine, Ellie,' I told her. 'And you're doing a good act of shivering.' And it's true. Her little knees were knocking away like anything.

'That's not shivering,' said Ivy. 'She's shaking because she's scared.'

'Scared of what?'

'Looking stupid!' said Ivy. 'Yesterday we had to pretend it's hot, and now today we're pretending it's cold. We'll never get away with it. Oh no. Oh no. Oh no . . .'

'Why not?'

Ivy stopped saying 'oh no' and was suddenly sensible. 'Haven't you noticed? The radiators are on

76

full blast today.'

Eh? I put my hand on the radiator under the mirror. **Oh no!** Sure enough it was baking. They were right, we were going to look a bit daft. Unless . . .

'You're fiddling with your hair again,' said Ivy.

'I KNOW I AM,' I said. Hmmm . . . coats . . . radiators . . . cold . . .? I found myself looking at the big old pipes that came out of the bottom of the radiator. They ran along the wall then disappeared down into the floor. Ooooooh . . .

'I've got it!' I told them. 'All of you, give me your water bottles, then get the Other Martha into class. Leave the rest to me and don't worry.'

'Are you sure we'll be all right?' asked Ellie nervously.

'Absolutely dead certain **100%** positive sure,' I said. Ellie gave me a little smile and toddled off with her knees not knocking quite so much. Gosh I'm such a liar sometimes.

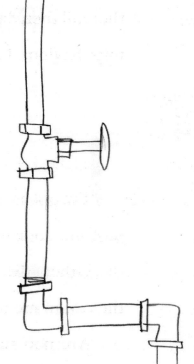

Mysterious Puddles

The reception area was like it always was in the morning with mums coming and going, saying 'hello' and 'see ya later', banging pushchairs together and dropping their shopping bags. Nobody noticed secret agent Agatha creeping along by the wall towards the radiator next to Miss Wizzit's desk. Oh, you don't know Miss Wizzit yet, do you? Like all school receptionists, you don't want to fall out with her, seriously you don't. Eeeek.

'The pile of head lice letters is over there on the far table,' Miss Wizzit was shouting at everybody. 'So if you need one, I don't want you coming anywhere near me.'

I got to the radiator. Nobody was

looking so I bent down and pulled one of the water bottles out of my bag and emptied it all over the carpet. It made a lovely big dark wet patch. **Perfect!** Job done, I shoved the bottle back in my bag and slipped away unnoticed like a shadow in a forest . . . **oooh!**

Next was the school hall.

Mrs Twelvetrees would be coming in to do an assembly, and there was a radiator right next to where she would be standing. I quickly tipped another water bottle out underneath it and got away as fast as I could. Next call was the radiator in the library, and then the radiator in the big store room. By the time I got into class I just had one full bottle left, so when I put my book bag away, I tipped it out under the radiator behind Matty's chair.

Ivy and Bianca were at their table with the Other Martha between them. They had set her up leaning forwards a bit with her hood pulled right over so it was hard to see the face. Everything seemed fine so far, but then Miss Pingle started to take the register. I'd forgotten about that!

'Darren? Liam? Alfie?' They each made their usual little grunty *here* noises and Miss Pingle ticked them off. 'Molly B? Bianca . . .?'

Miss Pingle gave her a funny look. 'Why are you still wearing your coat, Bianca?'

'Because it's cold,' said Bianca.

'Ex-CUSE me?' said Miss P doing a bit of teacher sarcasm. New teachers always do that, it must be something they learn at college. 'You all said it was hot yesterday and now it's cold today.'

Bianca looked at me crossly, because she thought I'd dropped her in it. OK, I suppose I had actually. Ellie was looking at me too and I thought she was going to cry. Oh well, if my plan was going to work it was time I got on with it.

'It WILL be cold,' I told Miss Pingle. 'Mr Motley is going to shut the boiler down because the radiators are leaking.'

'No one told me that,' said Miss P.

But then Matty jumped up from his chair. 'Urgh!' he said. 'The floor's all wet.'

Miss Pingle went over to look. 'Oh dear, I see what you mean. You might need your coats after all, but let me just finish the register first.' She continued reading out the names and everybody made their noises. Ivy looked at me as if to say 'What happens when she comes to Martha?' Good question.

I leant over and put my ear by the Other Martha's balloon head.

'Molly G?' said Miss Pingle

working through the list. 'Natasha? Ellie? Martha?'

'HA HA HA HA HA!'

I burst out laughing so Miss Pingle gave me a strange look. 'Sorry,' I said. 'It's just that Martha whispered something and it was a bit rude.'

'Did she really?' said Miss Pingle pulling a cross face. 'Well I'll thank you to keep it to yourself, Martha,' she said, then she ticked Martha's name off on the register just as I planned it! 'Leah? Philippa? And Donovan? Thank you class, now who wants to take the register to Miss Wizzit?'

I put my hand up. It HAD to be me, I had things to do. 'I just remembered I left my spelling book in my coat pocket,' I said.

'Then you better go to the cloakroom and get it,' said Miss Pingle. 'And could you drop off the register on the way?'

'Of course,' I said.

Ha ha, I'd fooled her . . . or had I? When I left the class Miss Pingle was giving me a funny look. No wonder! Why did I tell her I was getting my spelling book from my coat in the cloakroom? I was WEARING my coat!

I was going to have to be a lot more careful if my leaky pipe plan was going to work. I still had the trickiest bit to do.

The Emergency Mop and Bucket Operation

· ·

By the time I got to reception, the rush was over and Miss Wizzit was photocopying something for Miss Barking. I plonked the register down then pointed at the wet carpet. 'Has somebody spilt something?' I asked them.

Ho ho! Miss Barking immediately went to stand on guard at the edge of the wet patch. She held her arms sticking out to the sides to stop anyone getting near, even though the only people around were me and Miss Wizzit. 'Keep back!' she ordered us. 'You might slip and fall and hurt yourself. Miss Wizzit, can you organise an emergency mop and bucket operation?'

Miss Wizzit pulled the sort of face that you can only pull if you're Miss Wizzit and you're told to organise an emergency mop and bucket operation. She did a long yawn then she picked a walkie-talkie off her desk and spoke into it.

95

'Mr Motley, could you come and do a mop and bucket operation in reception?'

Motley's grumpy voice crackled out of the walkie-talkie. 'What for?'

'It's an emergency,' snapped Miss Barking.

'It's an emergency,' repeated Miss Wizzit into the walkie talkie.

Motley's voice crackled out again. 'Tell her to go and stick her head in a jelly.'

Miss Barking went red in the face, but she was still standing there with her arms out saving the whole world from the dangerously damp bit of carpet. She might be mad but she means well. Little round of applause for Miss Barking clap clap OK don't overdo it.

Meanwhile I went to check what was happening in the hall. Mrs Twelvetrees already had Motley lying on the floor next to the puddle, looking up at the bottom of the radiator.

'The radiator in our class has done that too,' I told them helpfully.

'So has the one in the store room,' muttered Motley. 'And now the one in reception.'

'And the one in the library!' said Miss Bunn sticking her head round the corner. 'I just came to tell you.'

'Oh golly,' said Mrs Twelvetrees. 'What a frightful bore.'

(Sorry I should have told you. Mrs T is the headteacher, very tall, plays cricket and tends to slap

people on the back when she's being jolly. She once did it to her husband at sports day and his false teeth flew out and landed in the sand pit ha ha!)

'It must be something wrong with the heating boiler,' I said. 'You better turn it off.'

'That will do thank you Agatha!' said Mrs Twelvetrees. 'I'm sure Mr Motley knows what it is.'

Motley thought very hard. He tapped the radiator with his screwdriver and wiped the pipes with his cloth. He rolled over and sniffed the puddle on the floor and then he sat up. 'It must be something wrong with the heating boiler,' he said at last. 'I better turn it off.'

'If anyone feels cold, they can go

and put their coat on,' I suggested.

'Agatha, that will DO!' snapped Mrs Twelvetrees. 'I'll make the decisions, now you go back to class. Oh, and tell Miss Pingle that if anyone feels cold, they can go and put their coat on.'

'That's a good idea,' I said. 'No wonder you're the headteacher.'

'Why, thank you!' said Mrs Twelvetrees feeling pleased with herself.

And I was feeling even more pleased with myself! They had both said exactly what they were meant to say. Gosh some days I'm just so brilliant.

☆ The Clever Dummy

Once we had got through registration and keeping our coats on, everything was fine apart from one little problem. The Other Martha turned out to be a lot cleverer than the real Martha.

The morning had started with

Miss Pingle giving us all a spelling test. Ivy and Bianca had got Martha's books open in front of the Other Martha. Ivy's really good at spelling and so she sneakily wrote all the answers into Martha's book at the same time as she was doing her own.

Next lesson was art, and that's Bianca's speciality. Everybody had to do a jungle drawing, then at the end they were all collected up and Miss Pingle looked through them. 'That's a really nice elephant Bianca,' said Miss Pingle. 'Oh, but look at this!' She held up a brilliant picture of a tiger up a tree. 'Who did this one?' Ivy glanced at Bianca who got hold of the Other Martha's arm and raised it in the air. 'Well done Martha!' said Miss Pingle. 'And you did it with your gloves on too!'

Next it was playtime. Everybody went outside, and me and Bianca put our arms round the Other Martha to take her with us as if she was walking. Ivy and Ellie crowded round so it wasn't obvious that the shoes were just dragging on the ground. We sat down on the bench with the Other Martha between us.

'It's numeracy next,' said Ivy. 'Miss Pingle's testing us on the six times table today. Does anyone know it?'

'Six times four is twenty-four,' said Ellie. 'That's my favourite because it sort of rhymes. And six

108

times six is thirty-six rhymes even more. And then six times eight is forty-eight so that rhymes too.'

And so Ellie ended up offering to do Martha's times tables test. Yahoo, go for it Ellie! After that it would be quiet reading time, then in the afternoon we were going to have a class history project. I couldn't see what could possibly go wrong but then . . . arghhhh panic panic! Guess what I saw outside the railings?

It was the real Martha waving at me.

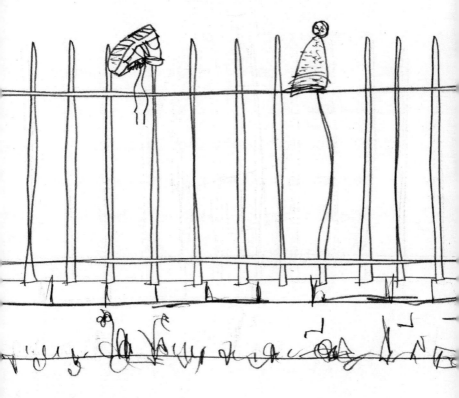

I ran straight over. 'Move you clot! Quick, go before somebody sees you!' We both ran along the railings until we got to the high wall at the end where we could whisper round the corner to each other.

'Why am I hiding?' asked Martha.

'Because you're already here!' I pointed at the Other Martha in the bright spotty anorak on the bench. 'You're supposed to be sick.'

'I'm better now,' grinned Martha. 'I'm meant to stay off but Mum's dropping me into school sometime after lunch because she's got to go out.'

'But you can't walk into class if you're already sitting there!' I told her. 'When you come into school, you'll have to hide in the toilets.'

'What, for the whole afternoon?'

'It's not my fault,' I told her. 'If it hadn't been for you and your pineapple and olives and octopus

113

paste . . .' Martha's face suddenly looked green again, so she wasn't *completely* better. 'OK OK!' I said. 'When you come in, get to the toilets. I'll try and switch you over. But now go, before anyone sees you.'

After playtime Ellie managed to stay brave and keep her promise to do Martha's times tables which was a bit brilliant. Halfway through she whispered to me:

'Doing this times tables test is THE most exciting thing I've EVER done in my WHOLE LIFE.'

YO! GO ELLIE! After that it was reading time so we just got a big book and propped it up in front of the Other Martha. For one happy moment I thought I could relax but . . .

Miss Pingle was sitting at the front marking everybody's tests and writing the results down in a big book.

She was making some funny little 'mmm' and 'ar' noises, but then she went 'ooooh!'

Miss P looked down again, checked some more results, then went 'oooh!' and this time she looked up and gave the Other Martha a long stare. Eventually she got up and started to walk across the room towards her. I had to stop her, so I jumped up to get a new book from the shelf which blocked her way.

'Sorry,' I said. 'Is everything all right?'

'Martha doesn't seem herself today,' said Miss Pingle. 'Her handwriting looks different.'

'Is that a problem?' I asked.

'No, not really,' said Miss Pingle. 'But she's also got top marks in all the tests.'

'That can only be because you're such a good teacher,' I said, but it didn't seem to work this time.

'Thank you,' said Miss Pingle. 'But if she's so good at tests, how come she's so bad at reading?'

'Reading?'

'She's been looking at that book for the whole lesson and she hasn't realised it's *upside down*!'

Oh no! How stupid was that? But then Ivy put her hand up. 'I'm reading mine upside down too,' she said. 'It's the new fashion.'

'Me too!' giggled Ellie. She was

really getting into this.

'Tee moo,' said Bianca. 'I mean me too.'

By the time Miss Pingle looked round the class, all the girls had sneakily turned their books upside down and even some of the boys had joined in. Of course most teachers might have got a bit strange at this point, but when you spend your Sunday evenings deciding what colour hair to have for the next week like Miss Pingle does, a few upside down books isn't going to rattle you. Miss P just went back to her table.

'You're mad,' she said as she sat down and doodled a few more ticks and crosses in our books. 'All of you. Mad mad mad.'

Big respect for Miss Pingle. She'll go far that one.

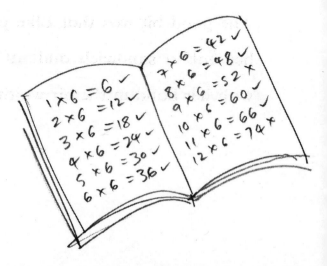

The Other Martha Puts her Foot in it

A t lunchtime the Other Martha decided to sit with us in the hall ha ha, of course she didn't have a lot of choice actually did she? The good bit was that Ellie passed her half a sandwich and sat there with her hand in the air waiting for

Martha to take it.

'What are you doing?' asked Ivy.

'Oops, sorry!' said Ellie and she blushed red. 'Martha always helps me finish my lunch. It's just habit.'

'You'd have been a bit freaked if she had taken it!' laughed Ivy.

While the others were finishing, I went off to see if the real Martha had arrived. She wasn't in reception so I checked all the toilets, but she wasn't there either, so I went out to find the others in the playground. They were all back on the bench with the Other Martha between them, but Gwendoline Tutt had decided to try to squeeze herself on too. She had her bully friend Olivia with her, although she isn't really a friend, they just hang out together because nobody else likes them.

'There's no room,' said Ivy hugging the Other Martha to stop her falling off.

'You lot think you're so clever because you're going on this trip, don't you?' sneered Gwendoline.

'Just leave us alone, can't you?' said Ellie which was pretty brave for her.

'Ooh, look who's bossing us around now!' said Gwendoline. 'Why should we do what you say?'

'Yeah, why should we?' laughed Olivia and she grabbed Ivy's arm and tried to pull her off the bench.

Ivy went a bit hyper waving all her arms and legs and everything so Olivia backed off and grabbed Bianca's coat instead, but Bianca slapped her hand away YO! GOOD ONE BIANCA. Then Olivia ducked down and grabbed Martha's foot, only it wasn't the foot, it was the shoe tied to the trouser leg. Olivia thought she was pulling Martha off the bench but the shoe came away in her hand and she fell

backwards and landed with a bump

on her bottom ha ha!

'Get up!' ordered Gwendoline crossly.

'But her foot came off,' gasped Olivia.

'Let me see that,' said Gwendoline and she snatched the shoe from her. I came running up from behind them and tried to snatch it back but Gwendoline saw me and ran off and there's no way I can catch her because she's got long skinny legs like a giraffe.

That left Olivia staring at our Other Martha who had a foot missing and a bit of newspaper poking out of her trouser leg. 'That's not Martha, is it?' she asked. And then before anyone could say anything she ran off shouting 'I'm telling Gwendoline!'

Miss Pingle was just coming out to ring the bell for the end of lunchtime so the only thing we could do was get the Other Martha back into class as fast as we could. Obviously all the other kids would know about her by the time lessons started. I just had to hope that the real Martha would turn up before the teachers found out. Hope hope hope.

It's Tudor Time!

• •

By the time we got back into the classroom, even the boys knew what was going on. They were having a laugh but were keeping it secret because they wanted to go and see the mummies just as much as we did. Most of us were still wearing our coats including the Other Martha

131

with her bright spotted hood. The good news was that Miss P had pulled the blinds down so it was a bit darker and it hid the balloon face better. What was even better was that Miss P was having another go with the electronic white board.

'Settle down everybody,' said Miss Pingle. 'This afternoon we're going to do some work on the Tudors.'

Wicked! We like the Tudors because they did lots of chopping off heads and things. It's a shame you can't book them to do parties. These days the Queen is only allowed to wave a bit when she goes out, so she must be a bit fed up even if she does charge £1000000000 to come to your church hall with a disco.

Anyway, Miss P pushed a button on her laptop and sure enough a big title came up on the screen saying *The Tudors*. We all gave her a little round of applause because she's rubbish at computers and it probably took her all night to get it right. She smiled and said, 'The first Tudor king was Henry the Seventh in 1485.' My my, how jolly interesting. 'Now then, can anybody tell me who this is?' She clicked the mouse button.

'Henry the Eighth!' we all shouted. We like him because he had six wives which is pretty good going for a big fatty who wore tights.

'Correct!' Miss Pingle was

starting to relax, and that's when the best bit happened. She clicked the mouse again. 'Can anybody tell me who *this* is?'

Ha ha ha ha ha ha!

'Yes Miss, it's your boyfriend Dave wearing funny shorts and eating an ice cream.'

'Eeeek!' said Miss Pingle blushing bright red. She wiggled the mouse around and clicked it a few times. We got a green triangle that said it measured 5cm along the bottom BORING then we got a map of Birmingham followed by a nice one of Dave and Miss P doing some **LONG KISSING. Wa-hoo!** Suddenly the white board went black because Miss P freaked out and pushed all the buttons on the keyboard at once. 'Oh dear what a pity it's broken,' she said. 'Never mind, we'll just try to act it out instead.'

Acting out the Tudors? Brilliant.

Miss P had found this old play about Henry the Eighth. It was called *Henry the Tudor Dude*. Matty got to be King Henry and Liam was the funny executioner.

'Who wants to be one of Henry's wives?' asked Miss Pingle. Ivy always wants to do acting parts, so her hand shot up in the air.

'Oh yeah wow me please wow yeah please me yeah wow please can I please please please . . .?'

'YES IVY YOU CAN!' said Miss Pingle otherwise Ivy would never have shut up. 'You can be Catherine of Aragon. And Martha, you can be Anne Boleyn.'

It was only then that we realised that Ivy had been holding the Other Martha's arm to keep her steady, and when she'd put her hand up it looked like Martha had put her hand up too. This was going to make things a bit awkward!

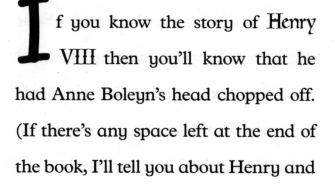

The Strange Story of Queen Martha

I f you know the story of Henry VIII then you'll know that he had Anne Boleyn's head chopped off. (If there's any space left at the end of the book, I'll tell you about Henry and

140

his wives because it's dead interesting and he chops his wife's head off twice. That's not the same wife by the way ha ha! The second one was a different one but they both turned into ghosts. How cool is that? You'll love it.)

Liam had got all excited about this head chopping business because he was the executioner. 'I can't wait!' he said. 'But how do I chop Anne Boleyn's head off in the play?'

'With this!' Miss Pingle held up something she'd found in the store room. *Ta-dah* . . . you should have seen Liam's face! He was expecting a whopping great metal axe, but it turned out to be about the size of a spoon, made of soft gold plastic and had *Pirate Pete* written on it. If Henry's axe had been like that, they wouldn't have needed to chop Anne's head off because she would have died laughing.

Miss Pingle passed the axe over

to Liam so he could have a practice swinging it round. Everybody was watching him, apart from me and Ivy. We were wondering what was going to happen when he had a go at the Other Martha? All we could do was play along and hope for the best.

While the others weren't looking, we bent the Other Martha over the table so the hood with the balloon in it was sticking over the edge. It looked exactly like Anne Boleyn would have looked on the chopping block, especially if Anne had been wearing a blue coat with yellow spots. Maybe she was? I don't know, they never tell you things like that.

'Anne Boleyn's all ready,' said Ivy.

'Thank you Catherine of Aragon,' said Miss Pingle and we all laughed a bit even though it wasn't all that funny.

The blinds were still down so I took the chance to pretend that it really was Martha for Miss Pingle's sake.

I bent down and said to the hood, 'Don't worry, we'll make sure Liam doesn't really chop your head off. You just make sure you lie perfectly still.'

At least that was the one thing that the Other Martha could do!

Everybody cleared a space as Liam came over with his axe. He raised it up ready to chop off Anne Boleyn's head. Miss Pingle passed Matty a piece of paper with a line for him to read out.

'Anne Boleyn, you have been

found GUILTY,' said Matty in a big king-ish voice. Everybody cheered **HOORAY** SUPER BRILLIANT GET ON WITH IT. 'Executioner, do your duty!'

'STOP!' came a voice from the doorway.

Oh potties. Not HER. It was just starting to be fun.

'Miss Barking?' said Miss Pingle. 'What can I do for you?'

Miss Barking walked straight up

to Liam and took the plastic axe from
him. She held it very carefully at arm's
length as if it was an old
smelly football sock.

'I was just coming to tell you that I'll be your second member of staff on the museum trip tomorrow. But there won't be any museum trip if this is what you're going to teach them, Miss Pingle.'

How **BORING** was that? The trip wouldn't be any fun at all if Miss Barking was coming.

'But it's only a plastic toy,' protested Miss Pingle.

'It shouldn't even be in the

classroom,' said Miss Barking passing it over to Miss Pingle. 'See it goes back to the store room now. While you're out I'll make something more suitable for you to use.'

Miss Pingle wasn't pleased at all, but Miss Barking was the deputy headteacher, so she had to do what she said. Once Miss Pingle had gone, Miss Barking made everybody stand back out of the way as she found two thin sheets of cardboard. She rolled one up into a tube and wrapped some tape around to hold it. Then she cut a blade shape out of the other piece and stuck it on the end. She held it up.

'There, children! It's completely harmless, but it looks just like the real thing.' Then the cardboard tube bent and the whole thing flopped over like a dead daffodil. Ha ha ha ha ha!

'How can I use that?' asked Liam.

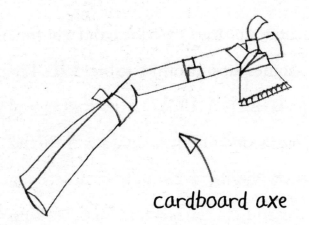

cardboard axe

'You just need to hold it properly,'

said Miss Barking. 'I'll show you.'

Miss Barking came walking over

to where me and Ivy were standing

151

next to the the Other Martha who was still bending over the table. **Oh no panic panic!** If Miss Pingle had found out about the Other Martha then maybe it wouldn't have been too bad . . . but what if Miss Barking found out? Eeeek! Ivy had her eyes clenched tight shut and all her fingers crossed and was muttering away in fear.

'Is she all right?' asked Miss Barking, pointing at Ivy with her floppy axe.

'She's . . . er . . . she's scared of your axe,' I said.

'Really?' said Miss Barking. She sounded surprised which wasn't surprising. Her axe must have been the must unscary thing ever, but what else could I have said?

'Yes really. It's so realistic. In fact maybe it would be better if we didn't do this. Can we just do some sums instead?'

Everybody looked at me like I'd just turned into a bit of old cheese.

'Eh? What? *Sums*? BOOOO!' shouted everyone else, and I can't say I blamed them.

'Don't you worry,' said Miss B. 'Martha will be perfectly safe so long as she keeps still.' She straightened out her axe, and raised it in the air.

'Now then Liam, watch carefully,' she said. Very slowly she brought the axe down so that it stopped just

154

above the neck. 'That's all you need to do, you don't even touch her. All perfectly safe.'

And that's when the brilliant bit happened.

The cardboard tube flopped again, and the blade fell on to the back of the anorak hood and knocked the balloon out on to the floor. Miss B was utterly freaked out. She stepped backwards and tripped on a chair and her big glasses fell off.

155

She blinked her eyes at the balloon.
She thought she was watching
Martha's head bouncing along with
the face turning to look at her.

'YOU CHOPPED MARTHA'S HEAD OFF!' we all shouted.

'What . . . how . . . why . . .?' Miss B's mouth fell open like a dead fish, but then it got even better because the balloon started to float upwards. Miss Barking thought Martha's head was flying round the ceiling, and it was still staring down at her.

'Arghh . . . no . . . make it stop . . .!' she was screaming.

And that's when the balloon
touched the hot light bulb and burst.

BAM!

'NOW YOU MADE HER HEAD EXPLODE!' we all said.

Miss B went all woozy and fainted and landed on top of Matty ha ha! All the others gathered round to have a look, but I grabbed Ivy and dragged her out of the door. I'd got an idea, but we had to act fast!

The Ghost of Anne Boleyn

. . . .

'What what what what what?' said Ivy who was still hyper-jumpy after that balloon had popped.

'We need to get help for Miss Barking,' I told her. 'Or at least you do. I'll see you back here.'

'Where are you going?' shouted Ivy, but I'd already gone.

Whizz zoom scamper scamper *phew*!

It was a close thing. I'd only just got back into class when Ivy turned up with Mrs Twelvetrees and Miss Pingle.

'What on earth has been going on in here?' asked Mrs Twelvetrees.

By now Miss Barking was sitting up but she was still a bit gaga. She pointed at the ceiling. 'Her head . . . bang!' Then she went digging into her big folder to find some instructions for when a kid's head

164

floats away and explodes.

'Whose head went bang?' asked Mrs Twelvetrees.

'Martha's,' said Miss Barking.

'You mean Martha Swan?' asked Miss Pingle looking at Martha's seat. The hooded shape in the blue and yellow spotty anorak was still lying face down on the desk. 'Martha?' said Miss Pingle. 'Can you hear me?'

The shape didn't move. Miss Pingle went over and took hold of the hood. Miss Barking was going into total panic. 'No . . . please . . . don't do it!' But then Miss Pingle pulled the hood back and Martha sat up.

'Sorry about that,' said Martha. 'I must have dozed off.'

Everybody had a good laugh apart from you can guess who.

'Argh! It's a ghost!' whimpered Miss Barking. 'I saw her head explode!'

Mrs Twelvetrees gave her a

headteacher-ish sort of look. 'I think you've been overdoing it. You better take the next few days off.'

So off went Miss Barking. She was looking a bit wobbly, but to be honest I was feeling a bit wobbly myself. After all, I'd just run all the way to the toilets and found Martha waiting there like we'd planned. If she hadn't been there, there would have been **MEGA TROUBLE**.

But then Mrs Twelvetrees had

bad news. 'I'm sorry chaps,' she said. 'I'm afraid this rather means that your trip tomorrow can't happen. You need two members of staff to go with you. What a pity. The mummies are soooo super.'

'Oh no, that's unfair! You promised and we want to go,' said Ivy. 'Can't you come with us?'

Mrs T shook her head. 'Sorry. I've got all the half-term reports to check. Miss Wizzit will never forgive me if I don't do them.'

But then the door burst open and in came Olivia and Gwendoline. They both pointed at Martha and said, 'That's not Martha!' which was a bit funny because anybody could see it was.

But there was no stopping Gwendoline. 'Here's the evidence,' she said and she plonked the Other Martha's shoe in Mrs Twelvetree's hand.

'What is this supposed to mean?' asked Mrs Twelvetrees.

'Her feet come off,' said Gwendoline. 'Show her Olivia.'

Olivia went up to Martha, grabbed her foot and pulled as hard as she could. Martha just held on for a while then gave a little kick and Olivia fell backwards and crashed into Gwendoline ha ha!

'That will DO!' said Mrs Twelvetrees sternly.

Gwendoline suddenly realised how stupid she looked so she turned on Olivia. 'You told me she was a dummy.'

'I thought she was!' said Olivia. 'Honestly.'

HA HA HA HA HA!

They both went bright red and stormed out of the classroom.

'What was all that about?' asked Mrs Twelvetrees.

'They were just jealous that

we're going on the trip,' said Ivy. 'Or at least we were going on a trip.'

That looked like it was going to be the end of it. Miss Pingle opened the blinds and we all had to straighten the chairs and tables then get our project books out. But Mrs Twelvetrees still hadn't gone yet. She was staring at the wet bit under the radiator, and then she spotted something on the floor and picked it up. It was bit of popped balloon! It seemed to have got her thinking, and then she started having a good look at the shoe.

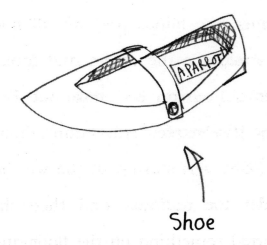

Shoe

Oh no, **eeky-freak!** Of course it was one of my old shoes and it probably still had my name in it . . .

'Is this yours, Agatha?' she asked.

I didn't have much choice did I? 'It might be,' I said. I was hoping she'd just pass it over but she didn't.

'Would you come to my office to collect it after school? There's

174

something I'd like you to help me with.'

Oo-er! But you'll have to wait for a few pages to see what that was all about.

Mummies and Ice Cream

'This is the coffin of Queen Parpunsniffet and it's 4,000 years old,' said Miss Pingle reading aloud from a leaflet. She was standing by a massive great big box with a really cool spooky gold face on it. YES! We had got to the

176

museum to see the mummies after all and it was completely brilliant.

'Let's move on,' said Miss Pingle. 'Now then, does anybody know what's wrapped up inside those bandages?'

Bianca's hand shot up. 'It's a bed doddy.'

'A bed doddy?' repeated Miss Pingle.

Ha ha ha ha! Hooray for Bianca. We love Bianca.

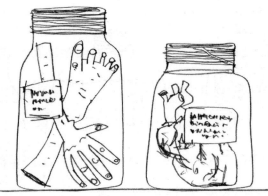

'She means a DEAD BODY,' said Ivy.

'Oh dear,' said Miss Pingle. 'I think a bed doddy sounds much nicer.'

After that we saw some strange

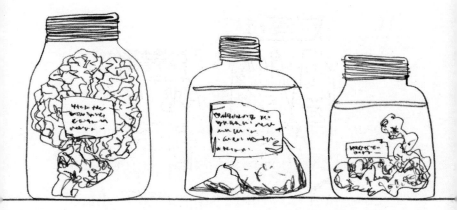

spooky statues, and the pots of bits of people's insides, and then the best part was the film showing how when Egyptians died they pulled their brains out of their noses with a hook before they wrapped the bodies up!

179

WARNING:

do NOT pull your brain out of your nose with a hook. Sorry I've got to put that in just in case you go round saying that this book gave you ideas.

When we'd seen everything (including watching the film THREE times yahoo we love it), we went out into the museum park and that's when something even better happened. There was an ice-cream van, and guess who treated us all?

'You deserve it chaps, I haven't had so much fun in years,' said Mrs Twelvetrees. 'And don't gollop down your ice cream so fast Martha! You'll be sick.'

'Me? I'm never sick,' said Martha and then she said 'OW!' because Ivy had given her a poke in the ribs and it served her right too the big liar.

Mrs Twelvetrees was lapping up

her own ice cream and it was dead funny especially when she said, 'Oh look chaps, Miss Pingle's got a little blob of ice cream on her nose!'

Miss P giggled and wiped it off with a tissue but that wasn't the funny bit. The funny bit was that Mrs Twelvetrees didn't know she had a great big white splodge on her own chin ha ha ha! She looked like one of those Egyptian man statues with a beard on it. Gosh, it was a lot better having Mrs Twelvetrees on the trip than Miss Barking, but I know what you're thinking. How come Mrs T could come with us? She was supposed to check the half-term reports, remember?

Top Secret Ending

• •

This last bit is supposed to be a secret between me and Mrs Twelvetrees, but seeing as you've read all this book, I'll give you a clue how she managed to sneak out to the museum. You remember when I had to meet Mrs T in her office after school?

Somehow she'd worked out the truth about the Other Martha, and she asked me to give her some help.

All the time we were at the museum, Miss Wizzit had been back at school sitting at the reception desk. She'd been staring at the door to Mrs Twelvetrees' office. Mrs T had specially asked not to be disturbed, but it looked like she'd been in there an awfully long time!

Miss Wizzit's a bit nosy, so

suppose she'd gone and had a look through the keyhole? (And I bet she did.) She'd have seen Mrs T sitting at her desk with her back to the door, checking the reports. So how was Mrs T able to be in the museum at the same time?

I'll give you a clue. The Mrs Twelvetrees in the office had her collar turned up and a big hat on. Oh yes, and there was a balloon involved but that's enough, now SHHHH!

Whatever you do don't tell Miss Wizzit. It's safer for all concerned if she never suspects. We'll just let her sit quietly at her desk getting on with some very important . . . er . . . well, whatever it is that school receptionists do all day.

There, you've just read a bit of **TOP SECRET** information, so don't let it sneak out. Don't leave this book lying open on the bus or anything. In fact it's probably safest if you just do what spies do and eat it. Oh no, here we go again . . . WARNING: *do NOT eat this book.*

Anyway, that's the end so I hope you liked it. Actually I was going to tell you about the time when we got Motley the caretaker to eat a million cornflakes ha ha! And then there was the time when Gwendoline thought Ellie was going on holiday to the moon, and then there's the time when James turned into a mushroom and there's lots more, but if we put all that lot in here then this book would be the size of a washing machine ha ha! So like I said, that's the end. Thanks for reading it, bye bye.

The End

x x x

(Actually it's not the end if you want to read the bit about **Henry VIII** and his wives which fills up the last pages. But if you don't then this IS the end so you can tick this book off and say you've read it WELL DONE have a gold star and a round of applause for YOU clap clap clap without stopping . . . ha ha brilliant.)

How did Henry VIII get through SIX Wives?

by Agatha Jane Parrot

1. Catherine of Aragon

Catherine was from Spain and to start with she was married to Henry's big brother Arthur but he died when he was fourteen which is a bit sad boo hoo. Then when Henry was king in 1509 he married Catherine instead. She had one baby girl called Mary, but Henry really wanted a boy which is a bit typical of dads isn't it? **So he divorced Catherine then he married . . .**

2. Anne Boleyn

Anne only had one baby and it was a girl too called Elizabeth which was no good. After three years Henry got bored of waiting, and he couldn't get another divorce so he played a very mean trick and had Anne executed in 1536. (Her ghost is supposed to haunt the Tower of London woo-hoo! Can't say I blame her, I hope she scared Henry

SILLY.) **Ten days later Henry moved on to marry . . .**

3. Jane Seymour

Poor Jane didn't last long. The good news was that she managed to have a baby boy called Edward the year after she was married. The bad news was that Jane got very ill and died about two weeks later. That was in 1537. **Henry was quite upset and waited more than two years before he married . . .**

4. Anne of Cleves

Henry saw a picture of this German lady called Anne and it looked so gorgeous that he arranged to marry her before he had even met her! But when she turned up in England he didn't think she was pretty after all, and even though she was very nice he thought she was a bit boring. He had to marry her anyway but he divorced her as soon as he could, although funnily enough they stayed good friends. **Two weeks later he married . . .**

5. Kathryn Howard

Kathryn was a lady-in-waiting to Anne of Cleves and she was really young and pretty and so fat old Henry married her as soon as he'd got rid of Anne. He was 30 years older than she was! Unfortunately

Kathryn also had some younger handsome boyfriends and when Henry found out he had her head chopped off in 1542 and she turned into a ghost too! **The next year he married . . .**

6. Katherine Parr

Katherine was nine years older than Kathryn Howard and at one point it looked like Henry might chop her head off too because she had the wrong religion. But Katherine had been married before and so she knew how to talk her way out of trouble. In the end Henry died in 1547 so she was the only wife that survived! But she's dead now of course otherwise she'd be about 500 years old.

Quiz question!!!

When Henry died himself, which wife was he buried next to? (Clue: she was already dead.)

The answer is Jane and they share a tomb at Windsor Castle and that's true so you can test people on that if you want. I tried it on Miss Pingle and she hadn't a clue ha ha!

Look out for

Agatha Parrot

and the Mushroom Boy

Helloooo! This story is about the time I was watching SING, WIGGLE AND SHINE on TV (the worst talent show ever WAHOO love it love it) but my evil brother James nicked the TV remote so he could watch football instead. Don't worry, I got my own back!

All it took was a giant yellow cake, some fairies, a school fete and a big sofa cushion. Oh, and Dad ended up with his toenails painted, so does that all make sense to you? It will do when you've read this book ha ha wicked!

Agatha Parrot